*For Tye, with extra sparkles*

First published in Australia in 2015 by Scholastic Press, an imprint of Scholastic Australia Pty Ltd.

All rights reserved. Published by Scholastic Press, an imprint of Scholastic Inc., *Publishers since 1920.*
SCHOLASTIC, SCHOLASTIC PRESS, and associated logos are trademarks and/or registered trademarks of Scholastic Inc.

No part of this publication may be reproduced, stored in a retrieval system, or transmitted in any form or by any means, electronic, mechanical, photocopying, recording, or otherwise, without written permission of the publisher. For information regarding permission, write to Scholastic Inc., Attention: Permissions Department, 557 Broadway, New York, NY 10012.

Library of Congress Cataloging-in-Publication Data

Names: Blabey, Aaron, author, illustrator.
Title: Thelma the unicorn / by Aaron Blabey.
Description: New York : Scholastic Press, 2017.
"First published in Australia in 2015 by Scholastic Press, an imprint of Scholastic Australia"—Copyright page.
Summary: Told in rhyme, Thelma the pony wants to be a unicorn—but when her wish comes true she discovers that there is a downside to fame, and realizes that she was happier at home with her friend.
Identifiers: LCCN 2016037157 | ISBN 9781338158427 (hardcover)
Subjects: LCSH: Unicorns—Juvenile fiction. | Ponies—Juvenile fiction.
Wishes—Juvenile fiction. | Friendship—Juvenile fiction. | Stories in rhyme. | CYAC: Stories in rhyme.
Unicorns—Fiction. | Ponies—Fiction. | Wishes—Fiction. | Self-acceptance—Fiction. | Friendship—Fiction.
LCGFT: Stories in rhyme. Classification: LCC PZ8.3.B568 Th 2017
DDC 823.92 [E]—dc23 LC record available at https://lccn.loc.gov/2016037157

10 9 8          19 20 21

Printed in the U.S.A. 88
This edition first printing November 2017

The artwork in this book is acrylic (with pens and pencils) on watercolor paper.

# Thelma
### THE Unicorn

# Aaron Blabey

Scholastic Press • New York

Thelma felt a little sad.
In fact, she felt forlorn.
You see, she wished with all her heart
to be a unicorn.

Her best friend's name was Otis.
He liked her quite a lot.
He said, "You're perfect as you are."

But Thelma said, "I'm not."

And that was when she saw it.
A carrot on the ground.
It gave her such a great idea,
she squealed and jumped around.

She took that simple carrot
and she tied it to her nose.
"I'll say that I'm a unicorn!
It might just work . . .
who knows?"

Well, as she did, a truck drove by.
The driver rubbed his eyes.
"Good grief! Is that a unicorn?"
he shrieked in great surprise.

As Thelma watched the swerving truck,
it very nearly hit her.
Would you believe that truck was filled
with nice pink paint and glitter?

Oh, Thelma looked amazing!
She was a unicorn.

"I'm *special* now!"

she cried out loud.

And so a star was born . . .

All across the whole wide world
her fans would cheer her name.

Thelma loved it! Every bit!

The FAME!

The FAME!

The FAME!

Thelma was a superstar!
Her dreams had all come true.

The Fairy Princess

But soon she found that so much fame
was kind of tricky, too . . .

You see, her fans were mad for her.
They'd scream and cry and laugh.
They'd chase her everywhere she went
to get her autograph.

In fact, they'd chase her all day long.

It NEVER

EVER stopped.

They chased her while she exercised.

They chased her while she shopped.

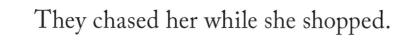

"Please don't chase me anymore,"
she asked the screaming crowd.
"We'll chase you all we want," they said.
"We're fans, so it's allowed!"

And some were not her fans at all.
No, some were really mean.

ROLLERSKATE
for
CHARITY!

And some just did the meanest things
she'd really ever seen.

I DON'T LIKE UNICORNS

I AGREE

So one dark night, she felt quite sad,
this famous little pony.
She said, "I thought that I'd feel great . . .

. . . but all I feel is lonely."

And so with that
she changed her mind,
this lonely unicorn.

She cleaned off
all her sparkles.

And she ditched her magic horn.

And then she walked right past the crowd.
They didn't even notice.

She thought how nice that it would be . . .

MARRY
ME,
THELMA

HELP
ME
BE A
UNICORN

. . . to see her lovely Otis.

And when he asked about her trip,
beneath their favorite tree,
she simply said, "Oh, it was fun . . .

". . . but I'd rather just be me."